The Ex Games

Part II

J. S. Cooper & Helen Cooper

Table of Contents

Chapter 1

My hands gripped the table as Priscilla left the room. I stared at her retreating back with hate. I'd known she was going to be a bitch as soon as I had seen her, and now, I knew I had been right.

Her words kept spinning in my head—fiancée, fiancée, fiancée. Brandon had a fiancée? I wanted to slap myself for being so stupid, so young and naïve still. I couldn't believe I had actually believed he had been referencing me when he'd talked about not living alone for much longer. I wanted to laugh and to cry at the same time. Idiot! I was an idiot. And all I wanted to do was run out of the building and never come back.

I knew as soon as he reentered the room, because the hairs on the back of my neck stood to attention and my body froze as if sensing some impending attack. He slid into the seat next to me and I felt his hand on my shoulder.

"Don't touch me." I glared at him.

"That's a first." He raised an eyebrow at me, mocking me with his gaze.

"You have a fiancée." I tried to sound calm and not as if I was about to lose it.

"And that's a fact?"

"According to Priscilla, it is." I studied his face, hoping to God that she had been wrong.

"What did I tell you about listening to other people?" He sat back and gazed into my eyes, and I couldn't stop myself from searching for the answers in the bottomless blue ocean that was his soul. "Remember, Katie. What did I tell you the last time someone told you something about me?" His tone was soothing, and for a moment, it as if he were my Brandon again, the man I loved, and more importantly the man who loved me. As I stared into his eyes, I remembered the day he had told me to not listen to other people.

"What's wrong, poppet?" Brandon stared at me curled up on the couch, crying, and walked over to me quickly.

"Nothing," I gulped, blowing my nose on my sleeve. I looked up through wet eyelashes and tried to smile. "Are those for me?"
"Yes," he nodded as he frowned. "A guy was selling roses on the street so I got you some. I'm sorry I'm home a bit late tonight. Work has been crazy."
"It's okay." I turned my face away from his as tears threatened to fall again.
"Katie, my love. What's wrong?" He sat on the couch and pulled my face towards him. "And don't tell me nothing, I can see from your tears that you've been crying."
"Are you cheating on me?" I whispered, barely able to get the words out.
"What?" He had an incredulous look on his face and I stared into his eyes to see if he looked guilty.
"Are you seeing another woman?" I bit my lower lip and played with the bottom of my shirt.
"What are you talking about, Katie?" He shook his head. "Where is this coming from?"
"I got a phone call." I was sobbing now, unable to hold it in. "Some lady told me that you were going to be late home tonight because you were going to be fucking her."
"What?" He looked at me in confusion, and I wondered if he had ever taken acting classes. "When did this happen? And do you have her number?"
"You don't have caller ID on the home phone," I sobbed. "And star 69 didn't work."
"Oh, she called the landline?" He sighed. "Not your cell?"
"Yes," I nodded as he pulled out a handkerchief and wiped the tears away from my eyes.
"Oh, Katie." He pulled my chin up to look at him. "I'm not cheating on you. I would never cheat on you. I love you."
"So who was that woman?" I still looked at him accusingly, though my tears were starting to dry up.
"Most probably one of my exes." He sighed and shook his head in thought. "You know I haven't been a monk. I've dated a lot of women in my life. And many of them wanted more than sex."
"So why didn't you give it to them?" I retorted, jealousy tearing through my soul as I thought about him with other women.
"Because none of them meant anything to me." His eyes pierced into mine and he just stared at me for what seemed like

5

hours. Finally he spoke again. "You have to know that none of them meant anything to me."

"But you were engaged once." I bit my lower lip, unable to stop myself from bringing up that last point. I wanted to be his everything. The only one he'd ever loved, but he'd been engaged before and I couldn't ignore that. "You must have loved her if you wanted to marry her."

"I was young." He sighed and caressed my cheek. "I was nineteen and thought the world began and ended with Maria." I blanched at his words and he grabbed my hands. "But it didn't. I was wrong. When we're young we think that love is this big grand emotion that will consume us for the rest of our lives. That's what young love is. That's first love. That's why it feels so good and hurts so bad."

"Do you miss her?"

"No." He shook his head and laughed. "Do you miss your first love?"

"No." I whispered slowly and closed my eyes. How could I tell him that he was my first love?

"Then you know what I mean, Katie. When we were eighteen and starting college, we thought the world was at our feet and the person we dated would be the one forever. We don't even know who we are then. When I dated Maria, I thought I wanted to be an artist." He laughed. "And you know I can't draw or paint for shit."

"You're not that bad," I lied.

"I'm worse than bad," he chuckled and leaned forward to kiss me. "I proposed to Maria because I thought that was what I was supposed to do to keep her by my side when she expressed an interest in a study abroad program."

"Oh."

"It worked." He kissed my cheek. "But boy, was it a mistake. I regretted it the moment the new semester started and she was nagging me to do this and that."

"But you wanted to be with her."

"My heart and the dream in my head thought I wanted to be with her. I wanted to get a relationship right. My dad, well, he's never been a stable one-woman man. I wanted to be different from him."

"Oh, I see."

"But I proposed to Maria for all the wrong reasons. We ended up breaking up four weeks into the semester."

"What?" I looked at him in shock and he laughed.

"And she keyed my car." His hand crept up my shirt and he gasped as he touched my naked breast. "You're not wearing a bra?"

"I didn't feel like it."

"You didn't go out like this, did you?" He pulled away from me, and this time it was he who had the jealous expression.

"What if I did?"

"I don't want other men seeing you."

"I had on a top, Brandon." I rolled my eyes. "I wasn't naked."

"But still." His eyes glazed over as he looked at my chest. "Men know."

"You're just trying to change the subject," I pouted at him and pulled away.

"Katie, listen to me good. I love you. I'm with you. Yes, I was engaged once. But only because I was young and dumb. I'm not a liar and I'm not a cheat." He paused and pulled me toward him. "I won't lie to you, Katie. Know that if there is someone else, I will tell you. Don't listen to anything you hear about me unless it comes from me."

"I just want to be your number one." I melted against him as he kissed me. I felt so loved when I was with Brandon, but I also felt so insecure. I always felt like one day I was going to wake up and he was going to be done with me.

"You're my only one, Katie," he whispered against my mouth. "The only one." He pushed me back down on the couch and pulled my T-shirt up. He kissed my stomach lightly and I waited in sweet anticipation to see if his mouth was going to go north or south. My whole body was tingling in excitement as I waited to see what he was going to do.

"Do you trust me, Katie?" He raised his head and I moaned aloud, disappointed that his tongue hadn't traveled to either part of my body.

"Yes," I groaned. "Of course."

"Let's go out."

"What?" I shook my head frustrated. "I don't want to go out."

"What would you rather do?" He smiled wickedly.

7

"I want to make love." I groaned and reached for him. "Make love to me."

"I will." He grinned. "Eventually."

"What do you mean eventually?" I made a face.

"Let's have some fun first."

"What kind of fun?"

"I want to take you somewhere."

"Where?"

"I can't tell you."

"Why not?"

"Because then it wouldn't be a surprise."

"You never said it was going to be a surprise."

"Well, I'm saying that now." He jumped up and pulled me up with him. "Come on, Katie."

"I don't want to go." I shook my head childishly and wiped my tears away. "Not unless you tell me where we're going."

"I want to take you to an art exhibit at the Met." He sighed and shook his head. "I wanted it to be a surprise because I wanted you to meet the artist."

"Oh." I made a face. "Sorry, I didn't realize."

"And I wanted to have sex with you behind one of the sculptures." He grinned at me with vulture eyes.

"Brandon," I laughed and jumped up eagerly. "Let's go."

"You're my eager beaver." He swung me around. "If I'd known you'd be this excited, I would have told you right away."

"I like trying new things with you." I paused and touched his face. "Unless we get caught. If we get caught, I'll kill you."

"Don't worry. If you get caught and you get a record and your job finds out and they fire you, you can just come and work for me."

"Yeah, sure." I pressed my face into his chest so that he couldn't see the rising red in my face. Every time he brought up my job, I felt a burning wave of shame and horror fill me up.

"We won't get caught though." He hugged me to him. "Go and put on a dress. Not too long."

"Okay." I grinned back at him wickedly, excited about what he had planned for us.

"Oh, and Katie?"

"Yes?" I turned back to look at him as I walked into the bedroom.

"No need to put any underwear on."
"Okay." I smiled at him and he winked back at me. My body rose in temperature and I giggled as I looked through all my new dresses, deciding what to wear, all thoughts of the phone call long gone.
"You look gorgeous." Brandon's eyes widened as I walked out of the bedroom in my flowy white dress and light pink lipstick.
"Your hair." He touched it lightly. "It's so wavy."
"As opposed to frizzy?" I smiled, joyous at the appreciative looks he kept giving me.
"I don't even know if I'm going to be able to leave the house." He shook his head as he kept staring at me. "Your breasts are telling me you feel the same."
"Huh?" I looked down and saw my nipples poking through my top. "Oh, maybe I should put a bra on."
"No." He shook his head. "I want easy access."
"But other guys—"
"Other guys can fuck off. You're all mine. If I even see one looking at you, they won't know what's hit them."
"Oh, Brandon." I rolled my eyes and rubbed his jaw line. "You look sexy when you don't shave."
"You like the stubble, huh?"
"Yeah." I nodded and blushed. "It tickles."
"Tickles?" He frowned, and then he grinned at me as he understood. "I guess it's a good contrast to my tongue."
"Yeah, the rough and the smooth turns me on."
"Katie," he groaned. "You don't want us to go out, do you?" He pulled me toward him and kissed me hard, pushing his tongue into my mouth and sucking mine as if it were his favorite lollipop. I reached down and rubbed his cock. It was already hard.
"I think you're the one that doesn't want to go out anymore." I teased him as I pulled back from him. I reached my hand down his pants and held him for a few seconds before slowly running my fingers down to his balls and squeezing.
"Shit, Katie." He groaned and closed his eyes.
"Shhh," I whispered, using my hand to unzip his pants and pull his now extremely hard cock out of his pants. "No one's going to miss us if we're a few minutes late." His cock sprang free and I allowed my fingers to trace a light line along his shaft

9

before squeezing the tip. I could feel Brandon's body tense up as he waited to see what I was going to do next. I smiled to myself as I dropped my fingers and walked away.

"Where are you going?" He slowly opened his eyes and looked at me in confused desire.

"I figured we should get going." I gave him a wicked smile and his face changed to one of surprise.

"You tease," he growled and chased me as I ran through the apartment. He caught up with me quickly and picked me up into his arms before running to the bedroom. He dropped me onto the mattress and I squealed as he lifted up my dress and buried his face in my wetness.

"I knew you were ready for me." His voice carried up to me as his tongue licked me. He gently sucked on my clit and I squirmed beneath him, wanting to feel his tongue inside of me. He continued his light licking with the tip of his tongue and allowed his stubble to graze gently against me.

"Oh, Brandon," I cried out as his tongue slowly entered me. I trembled beneath him and wrapped my legs around his neck so I could feel all of his face against my pussy. My fingers gripped his shoulder as my body built up to an orgasm. I closed my eyes in sweet anticipation as I felt myself about to explode and then he pulled away from me. "What? What are you doing?" My eyes flew open in disappointment. "Oh, Brandon. You can't stop!"

"Who's the tease now?" His eyes laughed down at me and he pulled me up off of the bed. "Now let's go."

"I hate you." I hit him in the shoulder.

"No, you don't." He laughed and grabbed my hand. "Let's go, Katie McHorny."

"Okay, Brandon McHard."

We left the apartment with glittering eyes and bodies filled with lust. My body groaned at me in frustration. It wanted a release so bad and it was all I could do to stop myself from dragging him down an alleyway and begging him to fuck me.

"Let's catch a cab." Brandon pulled me to the curb and stuck his hand out. We were lucky—a yellow cab pulled over immediately and we scrambled into the back seat. "The Met, please," Brandon told the driver, who nodded and drove off. Brandon sat back in the seat and looked out the window as I started to squirm. I couldn't stand that he looked so cool, calm, and collected while my body was begging for a release. I closed my eyes to try and stop my body from crying out.

"What's wrong?" Brandon whispered in my ear with a smirk in his voice. I turned to stare at him and give him a small glare, and I could see his eyes laughing at me.

"Nothing I can't fix." I shifted away from him and gave him a small smile.

"What do you mean?" His gaze questioned me and he gasped as he watched me pull my dress up. "You wouldn't." His eyes and his voice sounded shocked, and I just grinned at him as I closed my eyes and reached my hand in between my legs. My body shuddered as my fingers found my sweet spot, and I felt Brandon's body go still as he watched what I was doing. I leaned my head back, rested it against the headrest, and adjusted my position in the seat so I could give myself easier access. I moaned as I gently rubbed myself. I was still wet and my body was happy that it was finally going to get a release.

"What are you doing?" he hissed in my ear, and I opened my eyes slowly as I continued playing with myself.

"What does it look like?" I smiled at him, and his eyes stared into mine as my body trembled at my own touch. He moved closer to me as his hand met mine and pushed my fingers away so that it was my hand guiding his fingers up and down on my clit.

"I'm the only one who makes you come," he whispered into my ear as he increased the pace of his fingers. I didn't say anything. I was scared that if I opened my mouth I would moan or scream in ecstasy and I didn't want the cab driver to figure out what was going on. I nearly screamed when he paused and I looked at him in frustration.

"Just a second," he whispered and I saw him undoing his zipper. "Slide onto my lap."

"What?" My eyes widened. "Won't the cab driver notice?"

"It doesn't matter." He pulled me onto his lap and kissed my neck. "Oh, Katie. Stop tickling me."

I looked at him in confusion, but then I realized he was trying to vocalize a reason for being in his lap.

"You can't stop me," I giggled and almost groaned out loud as he lifted the back of my dress up and I felt his cock in between my butt cheeks.

"Move forward a little bit." He pushed me forward with his hands and lifted my hips up slightly. His hard cock slid into me easily as he sat me back down on him. "You're going to have to do the work here, Katie," he groaned in my ears as I started moving back and forth slowly. "Oh shit." His hands reached up and squeezed my breasts as I moved back and forth on his lap. His fingers squeezed my nipples and I increased my pace. I closed my eyes as we fucked in the back seat and my body shuddered as his fingers went from my breasts to my clit.

"Come for me, Katie," he whispered against my hair. "I'm going to come soon, but I need you to come for me first." The feel of his fingers rubbing against me and his cock sliding in and out of me pushed me to the edge, and my fingers dug into his thighs as I climaxed on him. I felt his arms tighten around my waist as his body shuddered and he came inside of me. He kissed my neck as we both sat back and tried to breathe. His fingers clasped mine and I leaned my head into his shoulder.

"You guys said you wanted to go to the MOMA, right?" the cab driver asked us and we laughed.

"No," Brandon finally spoke up. "You can just take us back home. Thanks though."

"I'm sorry we didn't make it to the museum." He smiled ruefully as we walked back into the apartment.

"Don't be." I tiptoed and kissed him on the lips. "I still had a good night."

"I think we both had a good night." He laughed and licked his fingers. "You know I love you, right?" He pushed me back against the wall and stared down at me. "I would never do anything to hurt you. I would never cheat on you."

"I know." I nodded breathlessly as I saw the intensity in his eyes.

"Good. As long as we are honest with each other, nothing can break us up. And I will always be honest with you, Katie. Remember, if you ever hear anything bad about me, don't believe it. Only believe it if it comes from me."

"Okay." I felt my heart bursting with love for Brandon, and I was about to tell him the truth about my age when he pulled up my dress. "What are you doing?"

"You don't think I'm done for the night, do you?" He grinned at me as his fingers found my sweet spot again. I closed my eyes as ecstasy filled me once again and all thoughts of telling him the truth fled my mind.

I shifted in my seat, feeling aroused again as I thought about that second encounter in the apartment. The sex in the cab had been hot and quick, but the sex when we got back to the apartment had been slow and sensual. So, so sensual. Brandon's fingers tapping on my knee woke me from my memories and I blinked rapidly, trying to focus on where I was. "So you don't have a fiancée?" I looked at him hopefully with my heart in my mouth. Maybe the HR bitch had gotten it wrong. Maybe he was still the decent guy I'd known. Maybe that's why he had said our phrase. If the words hadn't come from him, it wasn't true.

"No, Priscilla was right. I do have a fiancée and I was on the phone with her." His eyes stared into mine with a challenge. I knew what he was thinking: *What are you going to do about it, Katie?* I could feel in my bones that he wanted me to react.

"But..." I shook my head in confusion. "You told me I shouldn't listen to other people. You told me that if it doesn't come from you, it's not true."

"You shouldn't listen to other people about me." He shrugged. "But I'm here now and I'm telling you that, yes, I have a fiancée."

"How could you?" I gasped, my heart breaking.

"How could I what?"

"Sleep with me," I whispered, my eyes wide.

"We didn't do any sleeping."

"How could you fuck me when you have a fiancée?" I hissed at him, mad.

He smiled then, a wide, mocking smile. His blue eyes looked down at me in disdain. "Men with power, men with money, men like me... We can do what we want, when we want, with whoever we want. I wanted to fuck you." He picked up a napkin

and wiped his hands. "So I did." He turned away from me then and stood up. "Okay, everyone. Let's get back to work."
I sat there, humiliated, feeling like a slut. Once again he had made me feel cheap, like a piece of meat a dog had discarded. I listened to him talking, but I didn't hear the words that were flowing out of his mouth. As I sat there, I felt my body getting hotter and hotter. I couldn't stand it anymore. I had to leave. I didn't care if I got fired—I'd find another job. Nothing else mattered but my leaving the room, right then and there.
I jumped up as Brandon stopped talking and he grabbed my arm as I made to leave the table. "Where are you going?" His eyes were dark as his fingers pinched into my skin.
"I'm leaving." I pulled my arm away from him. "I'm not going to let you treat me like this."
"You're not going anywhere." He shook his head. "Not until I say you are."
"You can't stop me." I turned around and quickly walked out of the room. I could hear my heart beating like drums at a rock concert as I hurried out. People in the room were whispering and watching me, and I knew they were all wondering what was going on.
"Excuse Katie, everyone. She just got an important call. She'll be back in a moment." Brandon spoke up and I looked back at him with a glare. He faked a sympathetic smile and nodded at me. "Take your time, Katie. We'll be here when you get back."
"I'm not coming back," I shot back as I glared at him. I didn't care who heard me. I was done. He had no right to treat me this way. Let him explain my abrupt departure. I half-expected him to follow me out of the room, and I was disappointed when I realized he wasn't coming. I walked into the elevator and waited for him to rush out of the room and run into the elevator to stop me. Only he didn't. The doors closed slowly and the ride down seemed to take forever.
I pulled my phone out as soon as I walked out to call Meg. I needed to talk to her. I needed someone to remind me what a jerk he was so I wouldn't burst out crying.
"Hello?" Her voice was breathless, and my heart stopped beating.
"Meg, what's wrong?"

14

"I was fired." She burst into tears. "The law firm laid me off yesterday with no severance. They said that they couldn't afford to keep me."

"Oh, that's horrible." I leaned against the wall next to the elevator with my heart beating fast. "Can they do that?"

"Yes. I had no contract. I was an employee-at-will." Her voice broke. "I don't know what I'm going to do." She burst into tears again.

"You can just get another job, right?"

"They told me that they won't give me a reference." She sobbed hysterically. "I'm done, Katie."

"Oh, Meg." My heart broke for her, as I knew how happy she had been when she had gotten her law job.

"Thank God you have this position," she sobbed. "You don't mind covering the next few months' rent, do you? I'll pay you back as soon as I have a new job."

"Sure." My heart dropped at her words. How could I quit now?

"You don't even have to ask. You know I will always be here for you."

"How is everything with you, by the way?" She sighed. "Sorry, I completely forgot to ask if you'd seen Brandon. My mind was caught up in my own issues."

"It's fine," I lied. "I saw him, but for, like, a minute. I don't even think he recognized me."

"That's good, right?" I could hear her blowing her nose. "Hopefully you won't see him again. Then you can just come back home and forget about him again."

"Yeah." My voice was weak as I spoke into the phone. "Everything is going according to plan," I lied again. Nothing was going according to plan. Nothing at all.

I closed my eyes for a moment as I thought about everything I had been through, everything I had put into action, and my heart broke again. I'd made a big mistake, and once again I was getting burned.

"So I'll see you tomorrow night, right?" Meg's voice sounded a bit happier. "I'll cook pasta and you can help me look for jobs."

"Sounds like a plan." I cleared my throat. "But I better go now. I think we're starting up again."

"Okay, great. Thanks for cheering me up. I miss you already."

15

"You need to get a boyfriend." I laughed, shaking my head at her words. "You won't have time to miss me then."
"I'm working on it." She giggled. "Bye, Katie."
"Bye, Meg." I put the phone back into my pocket and pressed the elevator button again. I walked into the elevator feeling defeated, deflated, and devalued. I couldn't believe that I had to go back to that room and sit next to him. I never wanted to see him again. He had made me feel like a cheap slut once again and I hated him for it. I hated the man he now was. How could he have a fiancée and sleep with me?

The elevator stopped and I walked out, deep in thought. I had only taken two steps when I heard his voice against my ear as he pushed me up against the wall.

"What are you doing?" I struggled against him, trying to stop my racing heart from being so excited at being close to him again.

"I told you. You don't leave until I say." His eyes were dark as he looked down at me. His fingers traced the lines of my trembling lips. "Don't ever walk out on me again."

"Or what?" I squared my shoulders and looked back at him with fire in my eyes. This wasn't over. Not by a long shot.

Chapter 2

"So I'm looking for us to make a profit by quarter three." Brandon's voice was passionate as he talked about his plans for the company. "That means we're all going to have a lot of late nights." He looked around the room, and his eyes fell on me for a brief second before moving on. "Does anyone have any questions?"

"Will we be getting raises anytime soon?" a guy across the table asked seriously and some others nodded.

"Let's talk about raises when we actually start seeing a profit." Brandon's tone was brusque. "Anything else?"

"Excuse me, Mr. Hastings." Priscilla walked into the room and interrupted the meeting.

"Yes?" he snapped.

"Maria is on the phone again and she says it's an emergency."

"Okay." He nodded and jumped up. "Excuse me, everyone. I'll be right back." He walked out of the room, and I sat there in stunned immobility. Had Priscilla just said Maria? It couldn't be the same Maria, could it? Not the one he had been engaged to when he was in college? My heart started racing, and I felt like I couldn't breathe. All my insecurities came flooding back and I wanted to scream and shout. Had he lied to me before? Had he really always been in love with her? I wanted to cry and bury my face in a pillow. Maybe everything I had thought we had was false. What if I had just been someone to pass the time while he tried to forget about his true love, Maria?

I stood up quickly and walked out of the room. I needed to get some fresh air or I was going to cry. I knew it by the pain in my head and the tightness in my eyes. I rushed down the corridor and to the elevator. I breathed a sigh of relief as the elevator arrived and I ran out when I arrived on the ground floor. I hurried to the outside and was grateful that I didn't see Brandon as I made my way out. I took two deep gulps of air and pulled out some gum to chew to calm my nerves.

"Cat got your tongue?" His voice was smooth and melodic, and I jumped slightly.

"Sorry, I didn't see you there."

"I didn't know I said anyone could leave the room."

"I didn't know that we had to wait for permission." I shrugged.

"I thought you were going to quit." He changed the subject.

"I had a change of mind." I looked at the ground to avoid staring into his eyes. They still made my heart leap and sing, and my stomach was doing flip-flops as he stared at me.

"It's funny how that happens." He smiled at me and took a step towards me. "You look just the same, you know." He studied my face and then my body. "More of a woman, but just the same."

"I'm not sure if that's a compliment." I smiled and then looked him over. "You look the same as well."

"Now that's a lie." He laughed. "I'm greying now." He pointed to his hair and I noticed a few grey streaks. However, to me, they only made him look more distinguished and sexy.

"It doesn't detract from your good looks." I made a face at him and we both laughed.

"You always were the most honest person I knew," he said wistfully, and an awkward silence befell us at the irony of his words.

"I guess we should go back up." I put my gum away and started walking toward the main entrance.

"Wait." He grabbed ahold of my arm and stopped me.

"What?" I looked at his hand with a frown.

"There was a time when you didn't regard my touch as something bad."

"There was a time when you didn't have a fiancée when you slept with me."

"There was a time when I wanted you to be my fiancée."

"What do you want, Brandon?" I sighed and pulled away from him.

"I want us to forget our past. Let's move on."

"Maybe you should have thought of that earlier in the day."

"I can still feel your body shaking as I fucked you in the bathroom." He groaned. "It felt as good as I remembered."

"Stop it." I shook my head.

"Did it feel as good for you?" He wrapped his hands around my waist and pulled me toward him. "Did my cock give you as much pleasure as it used to?"

I remained silent as he whispered in my ear, his hands grabbing my ass. He stared into my eyes searchingly and I just stared back, unblinking.

"You're shivering." His lips neared mine. "You're shivering, but it's not cold outside." His lips lightly pressed against mine. "You're shivering because you want me to fuck you again."

"Get your hands and your lips off of me." I pushed him away. "What would Maria say if she could see you?"

"That's none of your business." His eyes darkened.

"You're making it my business."

"Are you single, Katie?" He cocked his head and his eyes studied my fingers as I nervously played with my hair. "From your reaction, it seems to me as if you're also seeing someone. Does that then mean that you're no better than me?"

"Matt isn't my fiancé." I shot back, though I did feel all sorts of guilty. There were many things Matt didn't know about me.

"I'm sure he would love to know that you don't feel you need to be faithful to him because he isn't your fiancé." He shook his head. "But I suppose you like to keep all sorts of things to yourself."

"Is it the same Maria?" I couldn't stop myself from asking. I had to know.

"Is what the same Maria?"

"Are you engaged to the same Maria you were engaged to when you were in college?"

"It's none of your business." He looked away then and my heart fell. In my heart I knew it was her. "What are you doing this evening?"

"Why?"

"I have a business meeting." He looked at his watch. "With some Japanese businessmen. They're bringing their wives. It would be smarter for me to go with someone."

"Take Maria."

"She's in New York."

"I see." I bit my lip. I wanted to know if he lived with her. I was annoyed at myself. There were so many stones I had left unturned. I shouldn't be this unaware of what was going on in his life.

"So, I'll pick you up at your hotel at seven p.m.?"

"I didn't say yes."

"You're staying at the Diva, right?"
"Yeah." I looked up at him in surprise. "How did you know?"
"Just had a feeling. How'd you like those purple lights?"
"Fine." I looked away again, feeling uneasy.
"I'll end the session today at four." He smiled and started walking back toward the entrance. "That should give you enough time to get ready and do your hair."
"Who says I'm going to do anything with my hair?" I raised an eyebrow at him.
"I'd rather you didn't, actually. You know I prefer it wild and crazy." He paused by the main entrance and opened the door for me. "Especially when you were riding me and climaxing. It made me feel like Tarzan, with my wild Jane." He whispered in my ear as I walked past him, "I miss fucking my wild Jane."
I ignored him and continued walking to the elevator. I was not going to let him intimidate me or make me feel embarrassed. He knew how to push my buttons and was doing everything he could to get a rise out of me. I smiled to myself as a plan hatched in my mind while I walked into the elevator. I would show him who could play a smarter game. I was about to call his bluff, and I was going to enjoy doing it.

***

I walked out of the elevator and into the lobby in a long red dress. It had a plunging neckline and a high slit. I wore the dress with pride, and I knew that my accompanying stilettos made me look hot. I was going for sex appeal tonight, and if the looks of all the men in the lobby were anything to go by, I had achieved the look quite successfully.
Brandon was sitting on a chair waiting for me, and my heart stopped when our eyes met. I saw the look of surprise, desire, and lust as he took me in. Then he smiled at me—a warm, gentle smile that reminded me of when we first met—and I was taken back to the days when we were friends and lovers.
"You look beautiful, Katie." He stood up and reached for my hand. "I see you're finding it easier to walk in heels."
"Not really," I giggled, already slightly buzzed from the two glasses of red wine I had enjoyed while getting dressed. "I may need to hold your arm as we walk."

"That's fine." He held out his arm for me. "I'll be your knight in shining armor. I'll be there to catch you if you fall."

"Thank you." I smiled at him and my heart constricted as I remembered the last time he had said those words to me. We'd been in Central Park on a picnic. I'd been expecting him to pull out a blanket for us to lie down under so that we could have a quickie, but he'd surprised me by pulling out some rollerblades.

"No way." I shook my head vehemently. "I have no balance. No way I'm rollerblading."

"Come on, Katie." He pulled me up. "It'll be fun."

"I'm going to fall."

"I won't let you fall." He pulled me towards him. "I'll never let you fall."

"I'm a klutz. Trust me, I'll fall."

"I'll be your knight in shining armor. I'll be there to catch you if you fall." He kissed the top of my head, and I could hear his heart beating as I laid my head against his chest. I looked up at him, and sincerity and love were pouring out of his eyes. I leaned into him and pressed my lips on his. Our kiss was sweet and special and filled with promises. In that moment, I knew that Brandon would always be in my heart and I would always be in his. We were connected as one.

"Then come on." I laughed and pulled off my shoes. "Let's go rollerblade before I change my mind."

And we'd spent the rest of the day holding hands and rollerblading through Central Park, and I hadn't fallen once.

"Shall we go?" Brandon smiled at me gently and I nodded. We made our way out of the hotel and I nearly tripped as he stopped suddenly. "I want to apologize."

"Oh?" My heart stopped as I held on to his arm.

"What I did today, it was wrong. I shouldn't have taken advantage of you."

"You didn't take advantage of me." I made a face. "I was willing and able to say no."

"I couldn't help myself." He sighed. "When I saw you in the elevator, I couldn't believe it. I'd been waiting for—anticipating, even—that moment forever. And I just got caught up in myself."

"I guess no one can say we don't have sexual chemistry."

"I want you to know something." He held my hands and caressed them. "I want you to know that what Maria and I have... It's not what it seems."
"She's not your fiancée?" I asked him hopefully, but my heart fell as he shook his head.
"She is, but it's complicated." He made a face. "So tell me about this guy you're dating. Did you say his name was Matt?"
"Yeah." I nodded. "He's a nice guy, very dependable. Seems to like me a lot."
"Really?" He frowned. "Close to engagement?"
"I don't know."
"Does he make your body tremble when he fucks you?"
"No." I sighed as I continued. "We haven't slept together yet."
"Oh." He smiled. "I see."
"We're waiting so that we can make it special. Relationships and sex are about more than some quick fucks," I said spitefully, wanting to hurt him.
"But sometimes the quick fucks are the best ones." His hands crept up my back. "Sometimes, you want your man to just push you up against the wall." He grabbed ahold of me and pushed me back. "Sometimes, you want him to take charge and slide his hand around your waist and push himself into you, so that you can feel his hard erection against your stomach."
He pushed into me then and I felt his hardness against me. I stared up into his eyes wanting to stop him but also wanting to see how far he was going to take this. He adjusted himself so that his leg was in between mine, and his cock was positioned by my inner thigh.
"Sometimes, you dream of your man bending his head"—his lips moved to my neck and his tongue trailed to my collar bone—"and lowering his lips." He kissed down the valley in between my breasts and I stood there, frozen, not caring if anyone was walking past us and wondering what was going on.
"Sometimes you want your man to show you who's the boss." His hand reached up my stomach and stopped right below my breast before slipping into the top of my dress and caressing my breast. "Because, Katie..." He looked up at me with a light in his eyes as he squeezed my nipple. "Women like to be possessed. They like to be taken. They like to feel sexy and sensual, and they want to feel loved."

He leaned forward and kissed me hard as his hand pushed the top of my dress to the side. He bent his head quickly and took my nipple in his mouth, sucking it eagerly and nibbling on it as he would candy. I closed my eyes as ripples of pleasure swept through me. My hands fell to his head and ran through his hair as he sucked. I let out a whimper as he released me from his warm embrace and then sighed again in relief as he transferred his lips to the other nipple.

I felt my knees buckling as his arm wrapped around my waist and held me against him and the wall firmly. His erection pushed into me even more urgently, and I reached my fingers down to squeeze it gently. I tried to unzip his pants, but he pushed my hand away and pulled away from me.

He looked at me and smiled. "You see, Katie? Sometimes the quick fucks are the most exciting and exhilarating. Sometimes they turn you on more than you seem to want to admit. Unfortunately, this is not your lucky night." His eyes mocked me as he moved away from me completely. "Tonight, you will have to hope that your boyfriend, Michael or Tad or whatever his name is, gets some gumption and makes a move soon. Because, little girl, tonight will not be the night that you get any from me, no matter how sexy your dress is."

I swallowed hard as I looked at him, completely dazed. I wasn't sure what had just happened. Minutes ago, he had been apologizing to me, and I thought we were finally going to put everything behind us. But yet again he had my head spinning in anger and my body aching for his touch.

I didn't say anything to Brandon as we walked to the restaurant. Instead, I just mentally confirmed my plan for the night. Brandon was right and wrong. He was right about the fact that sometimes a woman just wanted a man to take charge and take her, but he was wrong about the fact that he wasn't going to be fucking me tonight. If I had anything to do with it, I was going to have him shouting my name and begging me to forgive him for all the shit he had pulled on me. As far as I was concerned, he had gotten away with far too much. I wasn't a woman he could use and abuse like some pawn in a game of chess. He was about to find out that he wasn't the only piece of royalty on the board, and I was about to get into the game. And this time, I was playing to win.

Chapter 3

"*Konnichiwa.*"
"*Konnichiwa.*"
I stood there and smiled at the wives of the Japanese businessmen Brandon was meeting for dinner. I felt out of place in my revealing dress, as they were all dressed very conservatively. Their wives looked at me with polite smiles, but I could see the question in their eyes. *Is she a prostitute?* I was embarrassed for all of two minutes before I realized that ultimately it was Brandon who would look like the fool.
"They like you." He smiled at me as we walked to the table. He was back to being nice again, but I couldn't tell if he was being genuine or putting on a show.
"I feel like maybe I wore the wrong outfit for a business dinner." I made a face. "Sorry."
"Why are you apologizing?" He squeezed my hand. "You look sexy as hell, yes, but I'm not complaining. I like dining with a beautiful woman at my side."
"Oh." I blushed at his words. "Thank you."
"No need to thank me for telling the truth." He pulled my chair out as we reached the table and then sat next to me. "This is nice." He looked around the restaurant and smiled. "It's been a while since we've gone out to eat together."
"Yes, it has."
"This time you can even order alcohol if you want to."
"Funny." I looked away from him and he laughed.
"Don't tell me I can't make jokes about your age. Not after all the laughs you had on my behalf."
"What are you talking about?" I glared at him. "What laughs?"
"All the laughs you and your friends had when you told them what a fool I was for believing all your lies."
"I never thought you were a fool."
"I was a fool." He sighed. "I don't know how I didn't figure out you were eighteen."
"I guess I was a good actress."
"That's the problem. You weren't." He chuckled. "When I think back to everything now, it's all so clear to me. How eager and happy you were all the time to see me, how open you were with

your feelings. The fact that you were a virgin and the fact that you were always willing and eager to do whatever I wanted to do sexually."

"Not everything." I shook my head.

"That's true." He licked his lips as he stared at me. "I never got you to agree to anal."

"Would you like to see the wine menu?" A waiter appeared at our side, and I looked at him with a small smile while dying of mortification inside.

"Thank you." Brandon took the menu and opened it so we could both see.

"Mr. Kai, would you like me to order the wine?" Brandon addressed the only person in the business party who appeared to speak English.

"Thank you, Mr. Hastings. We would like that very much." Mr. Kai nodded and then spoke to the others rapidly in Japanese.

"I don't think I'm going to be able to help much," I whispered to Brandon. "I don't speak much Japanese."

"Your presence alone is enough." He squeezed my knee and smiled at me. I tried not to pull away from him, but every time he touched me, I felt like I was flying and it was hard for me to come back down to earth.

"I think we're all going to have a less fatty steak tonight. I'm guessing everyone will have a filet mignon, don't you think?" Brandon spoke out loud as he studied the wine menu. "So I guess I'll choose a bottle that has a bit less tannin."

"How do you know?" I asked, interested.

"I tried to be a sommelier when I was in my twenties." He looked up at me. "And I worked at a couple of wineries in Napa and Sonoma."

"I never knew that before."

"There are a lot of things you don't know about me, Katie."

"Have you decided on your wine?" The waiter reappeared, and I sat back while I waited for Brandon to order.

"Let's see. We're definitely going to go with a cabernet sauvignon." He studied the menu and looked up at the waiter. "Will you check and see if you have a 2002 Abreu cabernet sauvignon from the Thorevilos Vineyard Napa Valley in the cellar, please?"

"Wines in the cellar start at $500, sir."

25

"That's fine." Brandon shrugged. "That's the wine we want, if you have it. Two bottles would be better than one."

"I'll go and check now, sir." The apathetic-looking waiter's eyes lit up as he quickly departed the table.

"That's too much money." I whispered at him. "You can't spend $500 on wine."

"If they have a bottle, it'll be about $850, actually." He smiled at me and his eyes crinkled. "I have billions, Katie. There's no need to be worried. Consider it a catch-up drink for all those nights I took you out to dinner and you only got a water."

"Yeah, but we're not dating anymore."

"Whose fault is that?" His fingers caught mine and he squeezed them until I looked up at him. "Don't tell me what to do, Katie."

"I'm not telling you what to do."

"You made me lose control in my life once. I'm not going to let you do that to me again."

"What?" I frowned, but then Mr. Kai started talking about business, so I just sat back and smiled at the other women in the group. They smiled at me politely and I smiled back, not knowing what else to do.

The waiter hurried back to the table with a huge smile. "Sir, we've found two bottles for you. Would you like to do a tasting?"

"Yes," Brandon nodded and raised his glass, and the waiter popped the cork and poured a sampling into his glass. Brandon gave it a quick sniff, swirled it in his glass, and then sipped. He allowed the wine to sit in his mouth for a moment before he swallowed. "Delicious." He nodded at the waiter. "I like it a lot. The wine is deep, well-balanced, and complex." He turned to me. "Just like I like my women."

"So you two married, yes?" One of the women on the other side of the table leaned forward. "Happy couple?"

"Yes." Brandon nodded and I sat back with a fake smile on my face.

"She is younger than you?" Mr. Kai questioned and looked back and forth at us. I was surprised at the bluntness of his question.

"Much younger." Brandon nodded. "But what does age matter when it comes to love?"

Mr. Kai didn't respond but instead seemed to explain the conversation to the others at the table. Some of the women's eyes changed from polite to accepting and I realized, now that they thought I was the wife, everything was okay.

"What sort of business dinner is this?" I whispered in Brandon's ear. "Only one of them speaks English, and I can't imagine this is a setting where any deals are going to get made."

"The Japanese culture is different from ours, Katie." Brandon kissed my cheek as he whispered, "This may seem like an informal dinner to you, but it is also a vetting process. A process where they will evaluate whether I am someone they think they can trust."

"At a dinner?" I raised an eyebrow.

"Yes, at a dinner." He pulled away from me and raised his glass. "*Kanpai.*"

"*Kanpai.*" They raised their glasses and smiled back. I lifted up my glass and repeated the phrase they had used. "*Kanpai.*" I took a sip of the wine and immediately felt soothed. This was a good glass of wine, indeed.

"Enjoying it?" Brandon looked at me as I continued sipping and I nodded. "It's a very delicate wine. The blueberry, boysenberry jam, vanilla, licorice, chocolate, truffle, earth, and smoke scream from the glass, don't they?"

"I, uh, guess." I laughed. "I mean, I do taste some blueberry, I think."

"I'll have to teach you about wine one of these days." His eyes danced as I took another sip. "There's a vineyard in Napa, owned by some family friends, that I love. They have a castle, and I always thought it would make a romantic trip."

"It sounds like it." I smiled back at him, but I wanted to question him. Was he saying that because he really wanted to take me or because he was playing a role?

"How long you two been in love?" the one lady who seemed to know some English asked. I felt tongue-tied and nervous at her question. I was scared that it would be obvious to Brandon that I still loved him if I answered.

"I think I've loved Katie from the moment I first met her," Brandon responded. "My heart only began beating the moment I met her." He stared at me with love in his eyes, and his fingers brushed a piece of hair away from my face. "She was my angel. She found me at a time when I was in an emotionally bad place. She saved me from myself. Her love, her beauty, her kindness, her love of life—they saved me."

"Oh, Brandon." My heart melted at his words, and I reached over and grabbed his hands. "I feel the same way." I couldn't stop the words from gushing out of my mouth. "I feel like I was made to love you, that a part of you has always been in me, just waiting for us to meet."

The couples across the table stared at us, not really understanding what we were saying but feeling the love flowing between us.

"I knew you were the one for me in the very beginning," Brandon continued in a soft tone, but then his eyes hardened as they looked at me. "I think a large part of it was your honesty. I always knew that, no matter what happened, we would always have the truth. And I knew that nothing could break up a couple that has the truth on its side." He pulled away from me, still smiling, and I felt a deep pain shatter my heart as he hammered the nail in.

He was never going to forgive me. It didn't matter that it had been seven years since the lie. Seven years for him to get over what I had done. He was determined to continue making me pay for what I had done. Taking this job had been a mistake. Everything had been a big mistake. I lectured myself to stop trying to give him second chances and to stop hoping for the impossible. How much more did he have to tell me or do before I would accept that we were over forever? All I had left to do was to do to him what he had done to me. I was going to fuck him and then leave him as if he meant nothing to me. I knew that it might not break his heart, but it would definitely hurt his pride, and that was all I could hope for right now.

***

"Did you enjoy dinner?" Brandon was polite and distant as we walked away from the restaurant. The dinner had gone well, and his guests had gone off in their taxis looking fairly pleased. I wasn't sure if it was due to the wine or the company though. The two bottles of wine had turned to five, and we had all been a bit jolly by the end of the meal.

"I had a good time. They were nice." I walked slowly, trying not to stumble. He placed his arm in front of me, but I ignored it.

"Let me guide you, Katie. I don't want you to fall."
"No, thanks." I shook my head. "I'm fineeeee." My words
slurred slightly and I giggled.
"You're drunk."
"No, I'm not," I hiccupped.
"Katie." He sighed and pulled me toward him. "Hold on to me."
I wrapped my arms around him and pushed my breasts against
him as I let my left hand fall down casually and brush against
the front of his pants. His body grew tense as he held on to me
and I kissed his neck.
"Let's go dancing," I whispered in his ear, letting my tongue lick
his inner ear before I nibbled on his earlobe.
"You should really get home." He shook his head, but I could
see desire emanating from his every pore.
"I don't wanna go home yet." I hiccupped again. "Let's go
dancing. I know a place."
"How do you know a place?"
"I saw it yesterday." I grabbed his hand. "Please." We stood
there in the middle of the street, and he closed his eyes and
took a deep breath.
"Fine. We can go for an hour. That's it."
"That's all the time I need," I whispered to him as excitement
filled me. An hour was going to be more than enough time.
"Welcome to the club." A scantily clad lady ushered us into 'The
X Room' and I pretended that I didn't notice Brandon's look of
surprise as we walked into the dark club.
"Katie," he hissed as I dragged him towards the booming
music. "What sort of club is this?"
"I don't know," I lied. "I just want to dance."
"Katie." He grabbed my hand to try to pull me back, but I just
laughed and pulled away from him. I pushed my way through
the crowds of men until I found an empty booth in the side of
the room and sat down. "Katie." His eyes narrowed as he sat
next to me. "This is a strip club. We can't do any dancing here."
"Yes, we can." I moved into him. "I can dance for you."
"What do you mean?"
"I mean, I want to dance for you."
"Dance for me?"
"Or would you rather I said strip?"

"Katie, I don't know." He looked around and then back at me. "This isn't what I had in mind for tonight."

"Just because you didn't plan it doesn't mean it can't happen." As I spoke, I thought back to everything I knew about Brandon, and I realized that several things were starting to add up. "You like to be in control, don't you, Brandon?" I stood up and straddled him as I spoke to him.

"What man doesn't?" He shrugged.

"No, I mean, you need to be in control. Everything about you screams it." I shook my head in wonder. "I'm not sure how I never realized that before."

"I don't know what you're talking about."

"What was your life like before we met?" I pulled my dress up at the sides so that I could rub back and forth on him more easily. "I know you had lots of flings and you were focused on your job, but I didn't really know you." My eyes gazed into his as I kissed him lightly. He stared back at me with a guarded expression.

"It doesn't really matter now, does it?"

"It doesn't matter, but I want to know." I started unbuttoning his shirt and kissing down his neck to his chest. I gasped as his hand ran up my dress and grasped my ass.

"Hey, guys," A cute topless girl walked up to us. "You're welcome to do what you want, but if you want to remain in the booth, you need to order a bottle."

"A bottle of what?" I questioned.

"Champagne, Katie," Brandon laughed. "We'll have a bottle of Dom, please."

"Coming right up." The girl shook her breasts at Brandon and he smiled at her appreciatively.

"I can't believe you were staring at her breasts."

"What?" He looked at me with a bemused expression. "You can't be serious. You brought me to a strip club and now you're upset when I check out another ladies' tits."

"I'm not jealous." I bent my head and bit his shoulder. I didn't want to analyze my feelings too closely because he was right. I was pissed at the girl for flirting with him and even madder at him for seeming to enjoy the view. My inner brain was screaming at me, *She's the least of your concerns, Katie. He has a fiancée.* "It doesn't matter to me."

"Sure." He laughed and his expression seemed more relaxed. "Why don't you continue with your dance?" His hands pushed against my ass and brought me in closer to him. "Dance for me and I'll see how many singles I have."

"What?" I frowned as I realized that the mood had changed. I had gone from being in control and having the power to being his personal plaything. I knew that if I continued with my 'seducing him in the strip club' plan, I would be the one who ended up feeling hurt at the end of the night. I continued to grind back and forth on him and he reached up and pulled the top of my dress down so that my breasts were rubbing against his chest.

"Move a little bit faster," he groaned in my ear as his fingers slipped inside of my panties and rubbed me. "That's it." His voice was devious as he slipped his fingers inside of me. I continued moving, but I felt conflicted inside. I wanted him so badly, but not like this. Not with him calling the shots.

I jumped up quickly and rubbed my head. "I'm not feeling well." I made a face. "I'll be back." I hurried away to find the bathroom before I quickly washed my face with water and drank some to clear my head. I didn't know what I was going to do. My plan had been to pretend I was really drunk, take him to the strip club, fuck him, and leave. But it would only work if he wasn't the one in control. Now he was the one guiding me. He was the one turning me on. If we had sex in that booth, it was going to be him leaving me and making me feel guilty. I wasn't going to let that happen. Tears fell from my eyes as I stared in the mirror at my reflection. Who was I becoming? It was one thing for me to have this plan when I thought he was single, but now I knew he had a fiancée and I was still going through with everything. How could I do this to another woman? I took another gulp of water and walked back through the flashing lights, loud music, and naked women knowing I had made a mistake.

"Are you okay?" Brandon jumped up as soon as I reached the booth and he stared at me in concern. "What's wrong?"

"Nothing." I shook my head and avoided eye contact with him.

"What's wrong, my Katie?" He pulled me toward him, his fingers nudging my chin up to look at him.

"Nothing." I averted my gaze.

"Hey, guys. The Dom is here." The half-naked waitress came back and I wanted to groan.

"Set it on the table, thanks." Brandon's eyes never left mine. "Katie," he continued. "I know something is wrong. I can see it in your eyes. Tell me what's wrong?"

"I want to go home," I mumbled, my insides crumbling as he held me against him.

"I'm not letting you go anywhere unless you tell me what's wrong." His voice was adamant and he pulled me down to the couch to him. "Katie." His fingers caressed my cheeks. "Please tell me what's wrong."

"I'm just not feeling good."

"Do you need me to take you to the doctor?" His eyes looked worried as I shook my head. Why was he being so nice? He was making this so much harder on me. I didn't want to be reminded of how caring he was. "Need me to play doctor?" He grinned and I shook my head as he made a funny face. "'Cause I can play doctor, you know that, right?"

"Hmm, I think I remember you made a pretty good doctor once upon a time."

"I know. Once upon a time, I nursed you back to health and became the luckiest man in the world." His eyes caught mine and we just stared at each other for a moment. In that moment, I felt like the last seven years hadn't happened.

"I was very lucky that night," I whispered as he kissed my cheek.

"I was going to propose, you know."

"What?" I stared at him in shock.

"That was going to be my Christmas gift." He rolled his eyes. "Corny, I know. I was going to do it at my parents' house on Christmas Eve. I had it all planned."

"I had no idea." My heart raced as I stared at him. "You never told me."

"It wouldn't have been a Christmas surprise if I had told you."

"I'm sorry I lied." I looked down at my lap. "I guess I never really got to say it before. But I'm really sorry. I didn't mean to deceive you."

"Shh." He shook his head and grabbed my hand. "Let's go."

"But what about the Dom?"

"What about it?" He laughed and grabbed the bottle up before throwing some bills on the table. "We're taking it with us."
"Where are we going?"
"Back to my apartment."
"Oh."
"If that's okay?" he asked me softly, a question in his eyes.
"Yes." I nodded slowly. *Just one more night,* I thought to myself. I just needed one more night to get him out of my head.

***

His apartment reminded me of the one we had shared in New York. It had the same homey yet masculine feel, and I immediately felt at ease. We walked into the apartment urgently and our lips fell upon each other as soon as he closed the door. He picked me up and placed the Dom under his arm as he carried me.
"Where are we going?" I looked up at him as he walked past what appeared to be his bedroom door.
"To the guest bathroom. It has a bigger tub than in my room."
"Oh, why?"
"One of the best memories I have is of the time we made love in the shower." He grinned at me. "I've thought about it many times. I want to make some memories in the tub now."
"Oh." I blushed as he reminded me of the night we had made love in the shower. It had been during our experimentation stage and many sex toys had been involved.
"Come here." He pulled me toward him and kissed me hard. I lifted my arms up and he pulled my dress off before admiring my naked breasts. "Shit, you're sexy."
"You're not so bad yourself." I pulled his shirt off and then his pants. "You're not wearing any briefs?"
"I was hoping to have some fun tonight."
"You were?" I frowned at him. "But you said earlier that I was going to be disappointed. You said you had no plans to fuck me."
"I lied." He laughed and his eyes clouded over. "You don't have the monopoly on that, you know."
I leaned forward and kissed him hard, wanting him to shut up so he didn't ruin the moment. His fingers played with my hair

33

and then he slowly pulled away. "Don't pout, I'm just running the bath." He turned the tap on and then poured a liquid into the tub. It started foaming up right away and I grew excited. "Are you sure we're both going to fit?"

"Yes." He reached over, slipped my panties off, and then got into the tub. "Are you going to join me?" He smiled and reached a hand out for me and I took it gratefully. I stepped into the tub and stood there, not sure where to sit. "Sit on my lap." He pulled me down towards him and I sat with my back towards him. When he reached over and touched something, all the lights went out. We sat there in the tub in silence for a few seconds as the bubbles filled up the bath.

Brandon grabbed a washcloth and started bathing me. His hands rubbed my neck and my shoulders then fell to my breasts and my stomach. "Spread your legs. Let me clean you," he whispered in my ear, and he used the washcloth to wash my private area.

I melted back into him, enjoying the feel of his strong hands as they moved the warm, soapy washcloth along my body. I closed my eyes and rubbed his legs as he continued to clean me. I moaned as I felt his fingers replace the washcloth in his exploration. They moved up to my breasts before he squeezed them and molded them to his palms. He then pinched my nipples and started kissing my neck. I groaned as his fingers slipped in between my legs and he caressed my clit in the water. The feeling was intense and slightly different.

After a few minutes, I shifted in the bathtub so that I was straddling him. He took my breast in his mouth, and I reached down and held his cock still so that I could ride him. We both groaned as I slid down on his hardness in the water and started gyrating. My movements were stilted in the small space, but he used his hands to hold my ass and push me up and down on his cock. Our breathing was fast as we fucked in the bathtub and the water splashed over the side as we orgasmed together. I lay flat on him and he held me for a few minutes as our bodies continued trembling against each other.

"I think it's time for me to wash you again," he said softly and kissed my cheek as his hand grabbed the washcloth again. I shook my head and took it out of his hand.

"No, I think it's time for me to wash you." I smiled at him deviously and lowered the washcloth to his cock.

We left the bathtub about thirty minutes later and made love one more time before lying next to each other in the bed. I felt tired and confused. My heart was playing games with my head and I didn't know which side was up.

"I've really missed you, Katie," Brandon mumbled as he played with my breasts in bed. "I think about fucking your brains out all the time."

His words sparked something in me, and as I rolled out of the bed, Brandon sat up.

"Where are you going?" he mumbled as he reached for me.

"I'm going home." I stood there in front of him in all of my naked glory, feeling powerful and satiated.

"What?" His eyes narrowed, and he ran his hand through his hair before rubbing his chin. "Where are you going?"

"Back to my hotel room." I gave him a wide smile and then bent down to kiss him one last time. As I pulled away, I let my breasts rub against his arm and I pulled away quickly as his hand went to grasp my left breast.

"You can't go now," he groaned. "You're drunk. It's not safe."

"I'm not eighteen anymore, Brandon. I can handle my wine." I laughed and pulled on my dress. "I think I'll be fine getting home by myself."

"No." He jumped up and walked over to me. "I'm not going to let you leave."

"I don't think you get it, Brandon." I pulled on my shoes. "I'm not a damsel in distress, and I don't need you. Thanks for the fuck though. You taught me some new tricks." I smiled at him as I grabbed my handbag. "I think Matt will appreciate all the skills you've taught me when we finally get to make love."

His face turned murderous at my words, and I walked past him quickly, hoping to get out of his apartment with the last word. I felt high as I hurried to the door. I had done it. I had fucked him and now I was leaving him without a clue as to what was going on. I had taken what I wanted and now I was the one in control. I'd showed him that he meant as little to me as I meant to him. My hand reached for the front doorknob and I grinned to myself in excitement. This was match point and I was about to win. I had done it.

A second later, I felt his hands on my shoulders.
"What are you doing?"
I gasped as he pushed me against the door and moved in against me. He raised his arms above my shoulders and leaned against me, pressing me into the door, his body acting like a trap.
"I just told you, Katie. I'm not going to let you leave." His eyes glittered down at me and his hand slipped up my thigh through the slit in my dress. His fingers pushed their way in between my legs and worked their way into my wetness, rubbing against my clit before slowly entering me. My body betrayed me by buckling at his touch and my legs moved apart involuntarily as he fucked me with his fingers. "And I don't think you want to leave right now, do you?" he whispered against my whimpering lips.
I closed my eyes as my sudden and swift climax answered him. And once again he was in control.

***

"Good morning, sleepyhead." Brandon's smiling face was staring down at me as I woke up. I stretched in the bed and yawned.
"It's too dark out to be morning," I groaned and closed my eyes again.
"It's not too early for morning sex though." His hand crept up from my stomach to my right breast and I moaned as he pinched my nipple.
"Brandon." I rolled over toward him. "Not right now."
"I guess I'll give you a break." He laughed and pulled me toward him. "I guess we did wear ourselves out last night."
"Yeah." I smiled back at him and kissed him softly before freezing. This wasn't a dream. This was real life. I was in bed with Brandon still. Flashbacks of the night before came back to me—my trying to leave, his stopping me and fingering me to one of the most intense orgasms I had ever had. Going back to bed and making love again before falling asleep.
"I'm glad you decided to stay last night." His eyes glinted into mine.
"I didn't have much of a choice, did I?" I pulled away from him.

36

"You always have a choice."

"I wanted to leave last night."

"To go home and call Matt?" His eyes narrowed. "Were you going to tell him how you fucked me again, but it was all good because you were going to let him fuck you next, like some sort of sloppy seconds?"

"How dare you!" I slapped his face hard and then clapped my hand to my mouth in shock as I stared at the bright red fingerprints across his face. "Oh my God, I'm sorry."

"No. I deserved it." He lay back and sighed. "I should apologize."

"No, it's fine." I shook my head and lay back as well. "It was my bad. I wanted to get a rise out of you last night. I guess I was trying to play a game and it didn't go the way I planned."

"So you didn't really want to go?"

"I don't know." I shrugged and looked away.

"Maria and I have never had sex," Brandon blurted out, and he turned toward me with intense eyes.

"What?" I turned back toward him.

"We've never had sex." He laughed. "I know that's hard to believe."

"But you're engaged?" I stared at him, confused. "I don't get it."

"I did it to help her." He shrugged. "I can't really talk about it."

"Do you love her?" I whispered, yelling at myself for asking the question that plagued my heart.

"I don't love her." He shook his head.

"Oh." I stared at him with wide eyes. Where did this leave us? Was it possible that we had a future?

"I've missed you, Katie." He leaned in toward me, and his fingers ran through my hair and down my face.

"I've missed you as well." I reached over and ran my fingers along his lips. "I've thought about your face for so long. I can't believe I'm here with you right now."

"I need to have you again. I need to feel myself in you." He grabbed me and pulled me toward him. "Let me love you, Katie."

I nodded and he pulled me up onto my knees before getting behind me.

"I remember that you always used to love doggy style." He laughed as he positioned his already hard cock next to my

dripping opening. "I can go so deep from behind. It almost feels like we are becoming one."
"I know." I groaned as he entered me. "Oh, Brandon. Don't stop." I groaned again as he slowly slid in and out of me. "Please go faster."
"Do you trust me, Katie?" His hands gripped my hips as he increased his pace slightly.
"Yes," I moaned and closed my eyes as I fell forward slowly.
"Let me take you in a way I've never taken you before." He grunted and I cried out as he withdrew his cock from me.
"What are you doing?" I moaned, wanting to feel him inside of me.
"I took one of your cherries. Let me take the other one too."
"What?" My jaw dropped open and I froze.
"Let me love you, Katie." His thumb grazed my butthole and I jumped.
"I don't know." I shook my head and turned to look at his face. I watched as he took his thumb and sucked it. Then he lowered it back to my asshole and rubbed it gently. He rubbed my asshole and then down to my clit and back. My legs buckled every time he touched my clit and my nerves were on high alert as his thumb trailed back and forth.
I didn't say anything as he continued teasing me. He then reached his fingers in between my legs and his fingers played with my clit before entering me. I groaned as I felt a small orgasm shake my body. He withdrew his fingers and rubbed his cock with my juices. He pushed me forward and rubbed the tip of his cock along my slit to my butthole. I groaned as his cock rubbed against my clit and I pushed back into him, hoping he would enter me.
"Hold on, sweet pea." He kept teasing me. Then I felt the tip of him at the other entry. I froze as he slowly entered me. It was a weird and different feeling. I felt strangely aroused by the feel of him in a place I'd never had a man before. He groaned as he slid into me slowly.
"Fuck, it's so tight," he muttered, and I felt myself grow wetter at how turned on he sounded. "Oh, Katie. Fuck. I'm going to come." He moved faster and faster, and I gripped the bed sheets as he stole my anal cherry.

"Oh, Katie!" He shouted my name as he pulled out of me and entered my pussy again. "Oh, fuck," He groaned as he slammed into me, his fingers holding my hips tightly against him as he fucked me hard. "Oh, yes." His body shuddered as he came hard and fast, pulling out of me and spilling his cum on my ass and legs.

I collapsed flat on the bed and he pulled me into his arms as he spooned me. I fell asleep with a small smile on my face, feeling sore and happy. *He's never had sex with Maria,* I sang to myself. *He can't love her if they've never had sex.* And then I fell asleep.

The phone rang and woke me up, but I didn't open my eyes. I felt content and happy as I lay in his bed. I was hopeful for the future now. Maybe we really had a chance. I had given myself to him freely and let him do things to me that I would never have let anyone else I didn't trust do. Deep in my heart I knew that everything was going to be okay. Everything had worked out for the best. My perfectly orchestrated idea had gone according to plan.

"Maria, what's going on?" he whispered into the phone, and I peeked at him through my lashes. "No, I'm not busy." His words hurt me as I lay there, but I tried not to feel jealous. He didn't love her. He hadn't even slept with her. I had nothing to be jealous of. I had just given myself to him, trusted him. He would do the right thing.

"What happened to Harry?" His voice was sharp. "Oh my God," he gasped. "No, it's okay. I'm the boss. I'll explain. I'll be on the first plane home. Just tell him that Daddy is on the way. Give him a big hug and kiss from me." And then he hung up. I sat up then, my heart beating and my head pounding.

"What's going on?" I spoke up, and he looked at me in surprise. "I've got to go. My son is in the hospital."

"Your son?" My face paled as I stared at him.

"Yes, my son." He turned away from me and started pulling on clothes.

"I don't understand," I spoke softly, but I wanted to scream, *I thought you told me you never had sex with her.*

"What don't you understand?" His voice was annoyed. "I'm not a monk. I had sex. I wasn't wearing a condom. My sperm swam. I now have a child."

"But you said..." My words drifted off as he threw my dress at me.

"Get ready. We have to leave." He walked out of the room, and I stood up slowly, my heart breaking and my asshole a sore reminder of how once again he had screwed me over.

I slowly pulled on my dress and my shoes. I felt numb inside and out. This was worse than before. This time I felt like I would never get over the pain. I was forever ruined by this man, this man that I both loved and hated.

"Come on, Katie," he called out to me from the front door. "Let's go."

He drove me back to the hotel in silence and I jumped out of the car in a hurry, feeling like the world was about to end.

"Thanks for last night, Katie," he called out to me as I walked away. "It meant a lot to me." I increased my pace as I hurried into the hotel, and it took everything in me to not turn around and tell him to fuck off when he told me he would call me.

Chapter 4

Meg felt awful that I had stayed in San Francisco because of her losing her job. She knew as soon as I arrived back looking like the creature from the Black Lagoon that something was wrong. My eyes were bloodshot and I hadn't even bothered combing my hair. I knew that I'd looked like a mess on the airplane, but I just didn't care.

As I walked into the apartment and collapsed onto the floor in tears, I felt like my life was over. I'd only felt this way twice before, and both of those heartbreaks had been due to Brandon as well.

"Oh my God, Katie." Meg ran into the living room and fell to the floor to hold me. "What's wrong?"

"It was horrible," I sobbed. "Worse than I thought it was going to be."

"So he recognized you?" Meg's eyes looked worried.

"Yes." I nodded. "Right away."

"That's good then, right?"

"He was going to propose to me!" I cried, the tears escaping me fast and furiously now as my body shook.

"What?" Meg looked shocked. "This weekend?"

"No, silly." I stopped crying long enough to laugh for a few seconds. "He was going to propose the Christmas we broke up."

"Oh, wow. I'm sorry, Katie." She hugged me close to her. "That must have been hard to hear."

"I slept with him," I burst out. "And it was wonderful and I thought he still loved me, but I don't know that he ever really did."

"What? Of course he loved you."

"He's engaged." I jumped up and hit my hands against the wall. "He's engaged and I still slept with him. I feel so dirty. I can't believe I let him hurt me like this again."

"It's not your fault." Meg didn't try to stop me from hitting the wall, but rather she stood there waiting for the moment she needed to hug me again. "Did you tell him about…you know?" Her voice trailed off, and her words ignited more pain in my chest. A pain that had been long buried and we never spoke about. I shook my head slightly and turned toward her.

"I don't know how I'm going to face him at work tomorrow. I don't know what I'm going to do!" I cried out. "I hate him, Meg. He used me. He made me feel cheap. Even cheaper than when he dumped me outside Butler Library. I know I lied, but I didn't do it maliciously. I didn't do it to hurt him."

"He's obviously got other issues, Katie. I mean, he is starting to sound like a bit of a psycho. Let's be real here—you never really knew him. You didn't even date for a year. It was a whirlwind relationship. He was your first love, and he's turned out to be a jerk."

"Why would he treat me like this?" I sobbed. "He has a son."

"Oh." Meg's eyes widened and she held my hand.

"He told me he never even had sex with his fiancée, but they have a kid."

"Are you sure it's hers?"

"She's the one who called him and told him that his son was in the hospital. As soon as she called, he forgot about me. He dismissed me like I was nothing. And then he casually thanked me for the fuck."

"Oh, Katie." She shook her head. "If you don't want to go back, you don't have to. We'll figure something out. If I've got to break into my trip fund, I will."

"No." I shook my head vehemently. "You've been working on that fund since you were ten years old. I'm not going to let you use that money on rent."

"I'd rather do that than have you face him one more time."

I squared my shoulders and wiped my tears away while taking a few deep breaths. "Thank you, Meg." I squeezed her hands. "I'll see how I feel in a few days."

"So you're not going back to work?"

"Not tomorrow, I'm not." I sighed. "Let him fire me if he wants. I'm going to get in the shower now."

"Okay. I'll be out here if you need to talk."

"Thanks, but I'm feeling pretty tired. I'll probably just go to bed."

"I'm going to start looking for new jobs right away, and not just law jobs. I'll take anything. Just so we can pay our rent."

"Thanks, Meg." I smiled at her gratefully and walked to the shower in defeat. It was over. It was definitely over. Every hope and wish I'd had in the last seven years was gone. Brandon Hastings and I were never going to get back together again. I slipped my clothes off and got into the shower, allowing the scalding hot water to burn my back and hopefully wash some of my sins away. There were so many things I regretted about our history together. So many little pieces I would have changed. I thought back to his phone call and started crying again. He had a son. A baby boy that was probably his pride and joy. A child he loved with all his heart. A child who came first in his life. And it broke me. After everything, it was the news that he had a child that finally broke me down.

***

"Hello, can I speak to Ms. Raymond please?" a snooty voice asked as I picked up the phone.

"Speaking." I sat up in my bed and put the ice cream tub to the side, not wanting it to fall over while I was on the phone.

"Ms. Raymond, this is Priscilla calling from Marathon Corporation's HR department. You haven't been to work in three days, and you haven't called in, so we wanted to make sure that everything was okay."

"I'm fine."

"Then why are you not at work, Ms. Raymond?" Her voice was harsh, and I knew that if she could she would fire me on the spot.

"I don't know what to say," I replied honestly and laughed about what her reaction would be if I told her the truth. *I slept with the CEO, who's my ex, found out he was engaged and has a son, and he broke my heart again. Oh yeah, and I also let him fuck my asshole. Win for me.*

"Will you be coming in tomorrow, Ms. Raymond?"

"Doubt it." I grabbed my spoon and dug into my Ben & Jerry's. I needed a strawberry cheesecake ice cream fix.

"Ms. Raymond, I have to tell you that—" She paused, and I heard some whispering in the background. "One moment please."

"Katie." His voice was silky and smooth, and my heart flipped.

"Brandon," I replied softly, the ice cream in my spoon long forgotten as it dripped onto the bed.

"What are you doing?"

"Eating ice cream," I replied automatically and he laughed.

"Come into work tomorrow please."

"I can't." My voice shook.

"I need you on my team, Katie. Please come into work tomorrow."

"You hurt me," I whispered. "I don't want to see you again."

"Fight for it, Katie." His voice was urgent. "You worked so hard to get this job. Are you really going to throw it away?"

"I don't know what to do. I hate you."

"Think about what you really want." He paused and then continued. "Think about what's in your heart and fight for it. Don't just walk away again."

"What are you talking about?" My tone grew angry.

"I hope to see you tomorrow." His voice was soft now. "I hope you're the warrior princess I always thought you were." And then he hung up.

I lay back on the bed with my eyes wide and my heart beating fast. I was shivering even though it wasn't cold. I closed my eyes as I remembered the last time he had called me his warrior princess.

It had been a Saturday, and we'd gone to lunch at some cute chic restaurant in Soho. We'd shared a salad and a sandwich and had been playing footsie under the table. I'd been going on about some new book I'd read. I think it was *A Tale of Two Cities* by Charles Dickens, so it wasn't actually new—just new for me. I had never really studied much history, so I had been fascinated by the history of relations between France and England.

Brandon was a bit of a history buff, so he'd been telling me about Louis the Fourteenth and his wife Marie Antoinette when I saw the manager of the restaurant run outside and start berating two young boys who were going through the trash can at the curb. The two boys looked tattered and dirty and had taken food out of the trash can to eat. Without thinking, I jumped up and ran outside.

"What's going on?" I asked the manager and noticed that one of the boys was crying.

"These two thieves are going through the trash. They need to leave."

"Thieves? They look like they're seven or eight." I shook my head. "And they are stealing rotten food. I bet they're hungry. Are you boys hungry?" I gave them both a warm smile and they nodded slowly. "You should be giving them something to eat, not chasing them off." I glared at the manager.

"I'm not encouraging these hoodrats."

"Everyone is a human being and should be treated with dignity and respect." I glared at him, my voice getting louder.

"What's going on out here?" Brandon's arm slid around my shoulder and his voice sounded concerned.

"These two boys were going through the trash for food because they're hungry and he won't let them take the scraps." My voice was passionate. "I think he should be getting them food from the kitchen and he's not even letting them take the food in the garbage."

"I have a business to run. I can't feed every Tom, Dick, and Harry for free." He glared back at me.

"These are kids."

"I don't care." He turned around and walked back into the restaurant.

"Wait here with the boys." I looked at Brandon and then hurried back into the restaurant. "I'd like to order four sandwiches with four bags of potato chips, four cookies, and four bottles of water." I marched up to the manager. "And I want them STAT."

"Excuse me?"

"If you don't want me to start shouting and letting everyone know how greedy and uncharitable this restaurant is, you will get them ready now." I spoke calmly. "Don't worry. I'll pay for the food."

He stared at me for a few seconds but then turned around and put in the orders. I smiled to myself at my small victory and walked back outside with the bags of food as soon as I had them. The boys had huge smiles on their faces as they stood there with Brandon and even wider smiles when I handed them the food.

"Thank you." They grinned at me and Brandon and then ran off down the road. I watched them with slight worry. What was going to happen to them once the food was gone?

"You got them food." Brandon pulled me toward him. "I'm so proud to be with you, Katie. You spoke up for those boys like a warrior princess and then you went back and got them food. You're everything I want to be when I grow up."

"Oh, Brandon." I giggled as he kissed me. "I guess reading this book about inequality in France all those years ago and witnessing how it still goes on has gotten to me. Little kids shouldn't be searching for food in the streets. There is something wrong with that in a country where we have so much and people are literally throwing good food away. Yet those two boys aren't even allowed to rummage for the leftovers. It's wrong."

"I completely agree." He kissed the top of my head. "Never change, Katie. Never stop being my warrior princess."

I sat up in bed as I remembered that day. I'd been a different girl back then. I'd been fearless. I had believed that nothing could or would stop me from achieving all of my dreams. My life had changed after Brandon broke up with me. But it wasn't his fault that I had lost a part of myself. I had made those decisions. I was the one who was in charge of my destiny and life. And he was right. I had worked hard in college and grad school to get a job like this. Granted, this particular company had offered extra perks, but I still wanted it.

I still needed to prove myself. I had let Brandon win the game once before. I wasn't going to let him win again and kick me off the board. I jumped off the bed and walked to my closet. I was going to go back to work. I was going to leave all my personal feelings at home. I was going to show Brandon that I was the warrior princess he let get away.

***

Life is a funny thing. I went back to work the next day and Brandon wasn't even there. All the pep talks I had given myself hadn't even been needed. I'd felt tense almost all of the day until my immediate boss told me that Brandon was out of town. I didn't ask where or why or with whom. I was starting to realize that the less information I knew, the better it would be for me. The next day he wasn't there either, and then it was the weekend. By the time the next Monday rolled around, I was feeling more confident and sure of myself. Maybe he felt bad about what he had done and I would never have to see him again.

"Yeah, yeah, yeah," I sang along with the song on the radio that one of the secretaries was playing as I went through the sales figures from the previous week.

"Good morning, Katie." Three simple words stopped my heart. I looked up slowly and my eyes gobbled him in. He looked so smart and debonair in his navy pinstripe suit with his crisp white shirt.

"Good morning, Brandon." I nodded and smiled quickly. He walked into my office and closed the door.

"It's good to see you." His eyes surveyed my face, but I wasn't sure what he was looking for.

"It's good to be back. Sales are going great. Thirty-five percent increase over last year." I mumbled on about work, hoping that we would keep it professional.

"I noticed." He sat down in the seat in front of my desk. "You're doing a great job."

"I'm trying." I nodded and looked down. "How is your son?" I groaned inwardly as the words slipped out. Why was I doing this to myself?

"He's fine." His eyes shone brightly. "Thanks for asking. He fell off his bike and hurt his knee. Maria overreacted and took him to the hospital." He shrugged. "I guess her maternal instinct kicked in."

"I see." My heart broke at his words. He was finally admitting it. Maria was Harry's mother, so that meant that Maria and he'd had sex. He had lied to me. I stared at him and I wanted to shout, *How could you lie to me like that?* So easily. It burned in me that he had no shame about it and I realized that must have been the way he felt with me. Only a lot worse.

"He's a good boy." He stared at me intently. "A very handsome boy too. He has his mother's eyes and my hair." He laughed. "There's no mistaking he's my kid."

"Why's that?" I smiled weakly. "Because he's so handsome?"

"No, because he's into everything." He laughed. "He wants to know everything and do everything."

"He sounds like a good kid."

"He's the best. He's my life."

"You and Maria are very lucky to have him in your life."

"We are." He nodded and stood up. "I should let you get back to work. Come to my office around 11:30 a.m. I need to discuss some things with you."

"Sure." I nodded in agreement as he walked out the door.

"Oh, and Katie." He turned around and gave me a small smile. "I'm glad you came back."

I smiled to myself as he walked out of the room. I could handle this. Yes, the pain of hearing him talk about his son killed me inside, but I wasn't going to die. Eventually, it would get better. And I'd be able to work with him without always thinking of the what-ifs.

My phone rang then, and I grabbed it up without looking at the screen. "Hello?"

"Katie, where have you been? I've been worried sick about you!"

"Oh, Matt." I bit my lower lip. "Sorry, I've been busy with work."

"I haven't seen you in close to two weeks." His voice was accusing. "Can I take you out to dinner tonight?"

"Dinner?" I repeated weakly.

"Yes," he laughed. "It's what most boyfriends do every once in a while."

"Funny." I faked a laugh. "I guess dinner would be fine."

"Don't sound so enthusiastic!"

"Sorry, just been busy."

"I see. Well, I wanted to celebrate my promotion."

"Promotion?"

"Yeah."

"At the *Wall Street Journal*?"

"That is where I've been reporting for the last three years."

"Sorry, sorry." I rubbed my forehead. "I'm a little distracted. Congratulations. That is great news."

"So dinner and drinks?"

"Sure."

"Maybe we can go back to my place after and watch a movie." His voice was light. "And see where the night takes us."

"I guess so." I bit back a sigh. This was getting harder and harder.

"I'll see you tonight then. I'll text you the restaurant info."

"Sounds good."

"See you later, Katie."

I hung up and stared at the phone, feeling guilty. I felt awful about playing Matt, and I knew that I needed to break up with him. Dating him wasn't right and it wasn't fair. Especially seeing as I had essentially used him. Maybe that was why it had all blown up in my face. I'd been using people and lying for months. Even Meg didn't know the truth. I sighed and went back to the files. I was going to have to come clean and move on. I would dedicate my life to my job. That was all I had left right now.

***

"Hey." I walked into his office without knocking.

"Have a seat," he pointed to a chair and whispered as he was on the phone. "Bill, I understand that you think that Epsonal is worth five million, but I'm telling you it's overpriced. I will give you two million and allow you to keep a one percent equity share in the company, and that's only because I'm being a nice guy." He paused. "I have to go now, so think about it. You have twenty-four hours to accept or decline my offer." He hung up the phone and smiled at me. "Sorry about that."

"Are you trying to buy Epsonal, the electronics company?" I asked, frowning slightly.

"Yes, why?" He looked at me in interest.

"What you said was wrong. The company is worth at least twenty million—or at least it will be in a few weeks when the government awards them the military contract," I answered before realizing I had slipped up. I wasn't supposed to know about the military contract. No one was supposed to know. I only knew because I had seen the files on Matt's computer when I had been looking for something else.

"How did you know about the contract?" Brandon's eyes narrowed. "No one is supposed to know about that. Bill, the CEO of the company, doesn't even know."

"And you're using that lack of information to buy his company from him early." I shook my head in shock. "So you can get it cheap."

"That's how business works." He shrugged.

"But that's illegal. That's inside information." My mouth dropped open. "That's wrong."

49

"It can't be that inside if you've read about it somewhere." His eyes challenged me and I kept my mouth shut. There was no way I was going to tell him that I read it while snooping around in my reporter boyfriend's laptop.

"What did you want to see me about?" I changed the subject.

"I wanted to let you know that I am going to need you to start working nights." He leafed through some files. "You're the best manager I have right now and I need to work with you on some important projects."

"Okay." I swallowed hard as he undid the knot of his tie and pulled it off.

"Excuse me. There are some days that ties make me feel like I'm suffocating."

"No worries." I smiled weakly and watched as he pulled his jacket off as well. I watched as his chest muscles flexed beneath his shirt and shifted in my seat. He was so sexy. Just staring at him turned me on.

"I have a business trip planned for next weekend that I need you to come on."

"Oh?"

"It's in London." He smiled as I gasped. "I know you've always wanted to go."

"Are you sure you need me to go?"

"Yes." He nodded. "I'm very sure."

"I'll try and make it work then."

"Apologize to your boyfriend, Tom. I hope I'm not ruining any plans."

"His name is Matt, and no, you're not."

"Good." Brandon stood up, walked to his office door, slammed it shut, and locked it before walking back over to me.

"What are you doing?" I whispered as he stood in front of me, unbuttoning his shirt.

"Disrobing." He grinned and threw it on the ground.

"But why? I thought you told me to come because you needed to discuss something with me?"

"I do. I need to discuss how hot you are and how my cock is aching to fuck you."

"What?" My face heated up as my hand ran to his chest.

"I know you want me too." He pulled me up. "You can't deny the unbelievable chemistry we have, Katie."

"We shouldn't do this, Brandon." I shook my head and gasped as he grabbed my hand and placed it over his already hard cock.

"I'm hard just from looking at you. I need to be inside of you," he growled and his lips came down on mine softly, waiting to see how I would react. I was too weak, I couldn't resist him and I kissed him back passionately, opening my mouth to let his tongue in and sucking on it.

His hands worked their way under my skirt and he pulled it up so that it was sitting on my waist. His fingers slipped between my legs and rubbed me through my panties. I groaned at his touch and traced my fingers down his back and to his ass.

"Oh, Katie, I can never get enough of you," he groaned and ripped open my blouse, burying his head in the valley between my breasts before nudging my left bra cup to the side with his nose and then devouring my nipple. I moaned as my body arched towards him and he moved me back slightly and lifted me onto the desk.

I leaned forward, grabbed his belt, and pulled him towards me. His eyes darkened as I undid his buckle and unzipped him. His cock sprang out hard and proud, and desire sprung through me. I couldn't stop myself from running my fingers along his shaft and teasing him. I couldn't keep my hands off this man. Our sexual chemistry was too great. I closed my eyes as he pushed me back onto the desk and pulled my panties down to my knees.

"Sex in the office never gets old, does it?" he growled down at me as his fingers rubbed me gently. I moaned as he fingered me and then lifted my legs up to his shoulders. He pulled my ass down to the edge of the table and then slowly entered me. His cock drove into me slowly and his finger rubbed my clit as he slid in and out of me. I groaned at his touch—it felt too good, too intense. My body could barely stand how sweet the pleasure was that was building up in me.

"You feel so good." Brandon's voice was tense as he increased his pace. "Your pussy was made for me. Each time I make love to you, it welcomes me back with pleasure." His eyes glittered down on me. "I could get used to these office fucks." His hands reached up to squeeze my breasts and I held on to the table as he started moving faster and faster. "Oh, Katie. Fuck. I'm going to come." He groaned and my body started to orgasm in response to his words.

BANG BANG. The loud knocks on the door made us both freeze.

"Who is it?" Brandon's went still, his cock still in me as he paused.

"Daddy, it's me, Harry," a little voice spoke up and I sat up in horror. Brandon made a face before he quickly pulled up his pants and grabbed up his shirt.

"Just a minute, son," he called out and pushed me to the other side of the table. "Go under the table. Now," he commanded me and I ran quickly and hid under the table while Brandon quickly got dressed again.

"Daddy," Harry's little voice called out as he banged on the door again. "Let me in."

"Be patient, Harry. I'm coming." Brandon's voice sounded loving and patient as I listened to him throwing on his clothes over the loud beating of my heart.

"Daddy." The voice carried into the room as Brandon opened the door. "You took forever."

"Sorry. I was just finishing up something."

"We came to take you to lunch." The boy giggled. "And I want a burger."

"What do you say?"

"Please."

"Don't forget your manners, Harry." Brandon's voice was soft. "And I guess I can make time for a burger."

"Yay!" Harry ran up to the desk and my heart stopped still. What if he decided to sit in his dad's chair? What if he saw me?

"Come, Harry. Sit on the couch," Brandon called over to him, and I heard the boy's footsteps retreat.

"Can I get a toy today as well, please, Daddy?"

"We'll see."

"And some ice cream?" the boy continued, and I wanted to laugh. I also really wanted to see what Brandon's son looked like. His mini-me. His child. It made my heart ache, but I still wanted to see. I guess I wanted to torment myself with what could have been.

"Now, now, Harry. Don't you think that's expecting a bit much?" Brandon's voice was light and I could tell that he was amused.

"No."

"There you are, Harry." A female voice carried through the room and my heart stopped.

"Maria." Brandon sounded happy and not like someone who had nearly been busted cheating. "I was wondering where you were."

"You know your son." She laughed. "As soon as he's in the building, he's rushing to Daddy's office, and he doesn't care who he leaves behind."

"Sorry." Harry laughed and then mumbled something I couldn't hear.

"Shall we go then?" Brandon laughed. "I'm feeling hungry myself right now. Let's go get something to eat."

"Yay." Harry squealed and I heard him run out of the room. Then a few seconds later the door closed. I waited for about two minutes before I crawled out from under the desk and straightened my clothes. There were no tears left for me to cry, though once again I felt ashamed of myself. My heart felt heavy as I walked to the door and I knew what I had to do. I had to leave Marathon Corporation. There was no way I was going to be able to work with him and be okay. I had made my bed and now I had to get out. If I ever wanted to regain my sanity, I needed to get out now.

Chapter 5

"I'm not sure why you ever dated Matt," Meg said as she walked with me to the subway station.

"He's a nice enough guy." I sighed, feeling guilty. Meg didn't know the whole story, and I was ashamed of myself for keeping secrets from her.

"I know. He seemed nice," she agreed. "He just didn't seem like the sort of guy you go for."

"What guys?" I rolled my eyes. "Matt's the only other guy I've really dated, besides Brandon."

"I know, and it's time for you to finally move on." Meg stopped and turned toward me. "I don't want you to hate me for saying this, but I need to say it. What happened wasn't your fault. Yes, you lied, and yes, you were a dumbass, but you were eighteen. You made a mistake. You did what you thought you had to do. You were in school, Katie. Your life was just starting. I know it hurts like hell, and I can't imagine what pain you're going through, but you can't keep beating yourself up. You need to move on. Please, for the sake of your sanity, you need to move on."

"I know." I smiled at her gently. I knew how hard it was for her to talk to me like this. She'd been with me after the breakup and she was the only one who knew everything I'd gone through, everything I'd lost when the relationship had ended.

"I hope Matt doesn't cry when you dump him." Meg made a face to lighten the mood.

"That would be bad." I laughed. "But I think he'll be fine."

"And you're handing in your resignation tomorrow as well?"

"Yeah." I nodded my head assertively. "I need to move on, but I also need to be professional about it. I can't just sit in my room and pretend that life isn't still going on, just because I'm depressed."

"I'm proud of you."

"I couldn't do this without you." I squeezed her hands gratefully. "I'm so upset that we have to rely on your savings.

"Don't even think about it." She shook her head. "That's what best friends are for. I'll make more money. I'll be able to go on a trip another time."

"I love you, Meg."

"I love you too, Katie." She gave me a quick hug. "Now go break up with Matt gently while I go and try to get a job."

"Good luck." I grinned at her. "You'll be a shoo-in for the bartender job."

"Let's hope so." She groaned. "At this point, we just need money."

"You got this."

"Thanks, luv. See you later."

"Bye." I watched her hurrying down the street and said a quick prayer for her. She was hoping to get this part-time bartender job that had been advertised at the laundromat. The pay was great, and no experience was needed. If she got it, it would definitely help us as we both looked for new jobs. I took a deep breath and ran down to catch the train. This was it. My old life was about to end, and my new one was ready to begin.

***

I didn't have the heart to break up with Matt over dinner. It just seemed too cruel to congratulate him on his promotion and then dump him in the next breath. I decided to do it in his apartment, and then I'd come clean about everything. I wanted him to know what I had done and why, so he could understand that he had done nothing wrong. The reason I was ending things wasn't because I no longer liked him. It was because I was still in love with someone else.

We walked into his apartment and I watched as Matt hurried into the kitchen to get a bottle of wine. He seemed like he was excited, and I had a bad feeling that he thought that tonight was going to be the night that we consummated our relationship. He brought back two glasses of red wine and I took mine eagerly. I was going to need liquid courage to get me through the night.

"What movie do you want to watch?" He shifted closer to me on the couch and I tried not to recoil.

"Actually, I was hoping we could talk." I took a deep breath and he frowned at me.

"Sure, but what do you want to talk about?"

55

"It's over, Matt. I can't go out with you anymore," I blurted out, and I was surprised that his face remained the same. Even the expression in his eyes didn't look shocked or upset.

"I see." He nodded and sipped some more wine. "Why is that?"

I took a deep breath and let it out. "About seven years ago, I dated a guy. A successful businessman. I loved him, but things went wrong. I waited for him to come back to me and he never did. I tried to forget him, but I couldn't." I chewed on my lower lip as I continued on with my story. "About a year ago, I decided that I was going to try to see him again. Maybe get close to him, see if any of the old feelings were there. I wanted to see if we could give the relationship another go."

"Okay."

"I didn't want it to be a one-off encounter." I sighed. "I wanted us to be around each other. I wanted to see if perhaps we could make it work. So I started trying researching him. I found a lot of articles about him. Business stuff, you know? And I realized that the best way for me to get back into his life would be if I went to work for him. But I knew that he liked to flip companies. I knew I had to get in with a company before he did, so it wouldn't look suspicious. So I needed to get a contact, someone who knew a lot about business."

"And that's where I came in?" Matt raised an eyebrow and I nodded.

"Most of the articles I read about him were written by you. You seemed to have information that others didn't." I bit my lip. "So I orchestrated a meeting in the lobby of your office building."

"The classic woman-bumps-into-man-and-spills-coffee-on-him routine." He spoke slowly as he remembered our first encounter.

"I didn't mean to use you," I sighed. "I wanted to be friends, but you were so nice and it just kind of became a dating thing."

"So you used me for information?"

"I looked through your files on your computer." I nodded. "I saw a list of companies that you said this businessman was thinking of purchasing." I looked down at my lap, embarrassed and not wanting to say Brandon's name. "And I applied to all of them for jobs."

"So my information was right?" Matt asked eagerly, and I wanted to laugh.

"Yeah. I got jobs at three of the companies. I chose my position based on an article you were writing. I knew then which company he was buying, so I accepted the job. And I started working there a month before it was even announced that he was buying the corporation. It worked out perfectly. Even my best friend didn't know that I had taken the job there because I wanted to see him again." I closed my eyes as guilt racked my body. "But it didn't work out. It was a mistake. I shouldn't have done what I did. And I'm sorry. I'm really sorry if I've hurt you."

"I can't say that it feels great." His eyes were blank. "I never expected this."

"I'm leaving my job as well," I hurried out so that he knew that it had all blown up in my face. "I'm quitting tomorrow."

"What?" This time his voice rose and he looked worried. "You can't quit your job."

"I have to." I nodded and I jumped up as I felt myself becoming emotional. "I can't work with this man anymore. He's horrible. I can't do it. I'm quitting and I'm never looking back."

"Katie, please. I think you need to think about this." Matt jumped up as well and I could see worry in his eyes. "You seem to love this job. You can't just quit."

"I can and I am." I leaned over and kissed his cheek. "I need to go home now. I'm sorry. But I have to go." I hurried to the front door and opened it, feeling awful. My insides were churning with guilt and I rested my head against the door.

Matt had looked awful right before I'd left. He'd looked like his world was about to cave in, and that was because of me. I couldn't believe how badly I had treated him. And for what? I shook my head and sighed.

I had to go back and explain to him that it wasn't his fault. I didn't want him to hate me. I wanted him to know that there were things I had really liked about him. I didn't want to leave the apartment with Matt feeling like he'd been used. I'd felt that way before, and I knew how horrible it was.

I walked back toward the living room to apologize once again for how everything had gone, but he wasn't there. I walked slowly toward the bedroom, half afraid that I would see him crying or something. I knew he was a man, but I'd never really witnessed how emotional men did or didn't get at the end of a relationship.

I reached the door of his bedroom and stood in the open doorway. Matt's back was to me, and I reached to knock on the door to alert him of my presence when he pulled out his phone and dialed some numbers. I decided to wait until he was done with the call and just stood there for a moment.

"Mr. Hastings, please." His voice was worried and slightly urgent as he spoke. "Hey, Brandon. It's Matt. We have a problem."

The End

The final installment of The Ex Games will be out soon. To be notified as soon as the next parts are released, please join the Helen Cooper Mailing List or J. S. Cooper Mailing List.

If you enjoyed this novella, please leave a review and recommend it to a friend.

Other Books by J. S. Cooper can be found here.
Other Books by Helen Cooper can be found here.

I hope you enjoyed this book. You can like J.S. Cooper on Facebook here and Helen Cooper here.

Made in the USA
San Bernardino, CA
03 July 2014